Zinnia
and
Dot

wo hens, Zinnia and Dot,
lived in an old chicken coop.
Both were very fat and even more vain.
You would think that since they spent most of
their time alone, they would have been friends—
but they were not. In fact, they rarely spoke to
one another.

One morning Zinnia broke the silence. "My new eggs are the most bea-u-ti-ful in the world," she said with a long, slow drawl. "They are as smooth as silk."

Dot raised her chicken eyebrows. "No, no, my dear," she clucked, "*my* eggs are the most beautiful. THEY shimmer like pearls."

"But mine are like alabaster," said Zinnia.

"Mine are as pure as the new-fallen snow," crooned Dot.

On and on the hens fussed, each insisting she had the loveliest, most brilliant, most perfect eggs.

"Of course, my chicks will hatch to be as gorgeous as their mother," Dot said at last. She jumped to the coop floor and strutted in the sunlight.

Zinnia was not to be outdone. She fluttered across the hay, displaying her brilliant feathers. "What beautiful chicks *I* will have," she said.

The hens were so busy admiring themselves that they did not notice who sat at the chicken coop window. It was a weasel.

Passing by, he had heard the bragging hens and stopped to see what might develop. All happened just as he hoped, and the weasel now saw his chance.

C R A S H ! The weasel burst in the window. Wildly racing through the chicken coop, he overturned nests and scattered straw. It was poultry pandemonium.

Then, just as suddenly as the weasel had appeared, he was gone.

Zinnia and Dot picked themselves up. The air was perfectly still. All seemed to be as it was before—but returning to their nests, the two hens gasped.

Their eggs were gone.

"This is all *your* fault!" each hen accused the other.

"*You* were the one who started it all!" Dot shouted.

"I never would have left my nest if you hadn't been showing off!" Zinnia shot back.

Behind them there was a gentle *bump* and the sound of something rolling. Zinnia and Dot turned around. There, in the middle of the floor, was one last egg.

Two chicken voices shrieked at once. "That's *my* egg!"

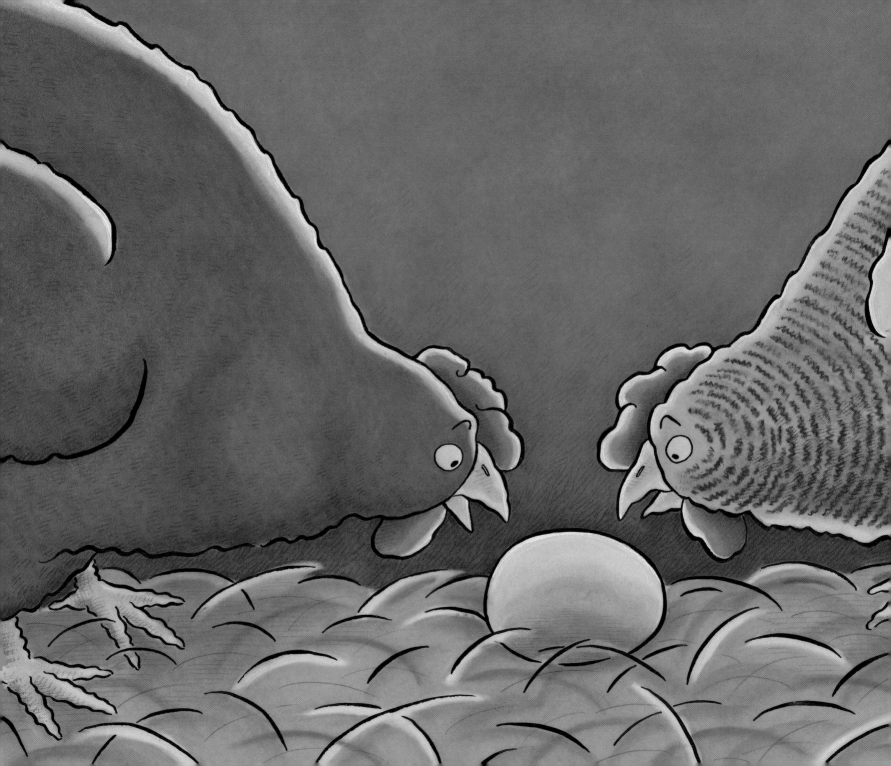

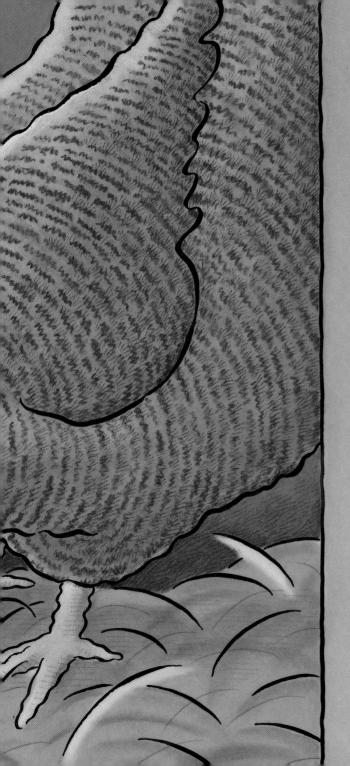

What a fight now began!

Zinnia knew without a doubt that it was *her* egg; Dot was just as certain that it was *hers*. Each refused to admit that the egg could possibly belong to the other.

Finally two mourning doves at the window interrupted.

"Please!" called one of the doves. "That poor egg is getting cold. If you don't come to an agreement soon, there will be no chick to argue over. Maybe you could share it."

Dot and Zinnia eyed each other suspiciously. SHARE? Never! Still, the egg *was* getting cold.

"Fine," Zinnia said. "I will sit on it first, and then you may."

"No, me first," said Dot, "*then* you."

Sharing was not something that either Zinnia or Dot did well.

"When the egg hatches, the baby chick will look just like me," Dot declared. "*Then* we will know whose egg it is."

"Yes, we will know," Zinnia snapped. "But it will look like *me*, because it is my egg."

Finally even these two grew weary of quarreling, each knowing that nothing would ever change the other's mind. An icy silence filled the air.

Days passed.

The mourning doves sometimes stopped by the chicken coop to see how the hatching was progressing.

There Zinnia and Dot sat, unmoving, refusing to even acknowledge that the other was there.

"Why not entertain one another?" suggested one dove. "Sing some songs, tell some stories."

"Ha!" cried Zinnia. "The only story I'll tell is about me and my baby chick *leaving* this coop!"

"Oh, *no*," Dot hissed back. "I will be the one leaving with *my* baby chick."

Again the hens sat in silence, brooding over what lay ahead.

Now, all this time, the weasel had been thinking about just one thing: the egg he left behind. And the longer he thought about it, the more he could not rest until he had returned to claim it.

"While I'm there, I might as well eat those two old hens," he growled, setting out for the chicken coop.

The two old hens, meanwhile, grew more irritable with each passing second. They only spoke to complain.

"Stop humming!"

"Stop wiggling!"

"Move over!"

Tempers were short.

And that is when the fly buzzed through the broken window. "BZZZZZZzzzzzzzzzZZZZZZZZZ zzzzzzzzzZZZZZZZZZzzzzzzzzzZZZZZZzzzzzzzzz . . ." Around and around and around he buzzed, again and again, until each hen thought she would scream. When the fly buzzed past Dot's beak, Zinnia FLUNG out her wing.

Zinnia missed the fly. Zinnia hit Dot.

"That *does* it!" Dot shouted. She jumped to the floor, dragging Zinnia with her.

The weasel saw his chance.

C R A S H ! Through the window he came.
At first Dot and Zinnia froze. Then they
turned on the weasel.

"Stop him!" shouted Dot.

"Don't let him near the nest!" screeched Zinnia.

One jumped on the weasel's back, the other
on his head. They seemed all beaks and claws.

Squawk! Cluck! Yelp!

The weasel leapt and rolled and snapped,
but he could not get rid of the battling chickens.

He struggled back to the broken window,
jumped out, and disappeared.

The exhausted hens collapsed on the coop floor.

"We did it," Dot said. "We scared the weasel away."

Zinnia shook her head. "Who would have thought we could be so brave?"

The hens, giddy from their victory, cackled as they sat back down on their nest.

"One hen could never have done it," declared Dot.

For once Zinnia agreed. "Lucky we both were here," she said.

The thought made both hens cackle again, so hard they cried.

"Shhhh! Listen!" Dot whispered.

A tiny *tap-tap-tap* could be heard underneath them.

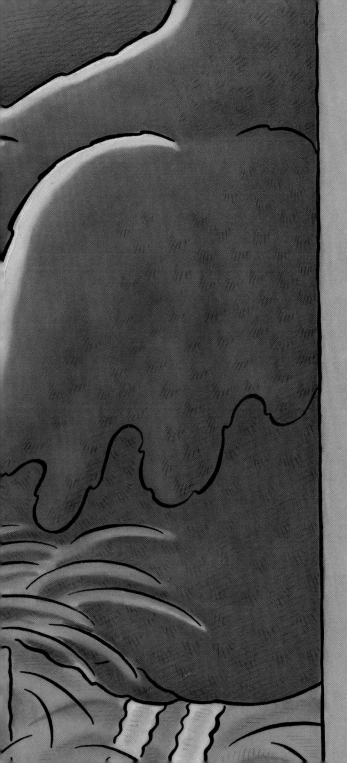

"Our egg!" they shouted.

Dot and Zinnia huddled at the edge of the nest, watching. First, tiny cracks appeared on the egg. Time passed. The hours seemed like days.

At last pieces of shell fell off one at a time, and finally the egg fell apart.

A wet, bony, very naked-looking baby chick emerged.

"He's bea-u-ti-ful!" gasped Zinnia.

"He's gorgeous!" agreed Dot.

Zinnia leaned closer. "His beak looks just like yours," she declared.

"But his feet look just like yours," insisted Dot.

The baby chick cheeped back at the four eyes above him.

"He's perfect!" Dot and Zinnia sang.

Never before was a baby chick so loved,
growing up with not one, but two mother hens.

That's not to say Zinnia and Dot always got
along. They didn't. But they did learn to be
friends.

And on the most important thing—their
baby—they agreed one hundred percent: he was
the loveliest, most brilliant, most perfect chick
in the world.

And that was all that really mattered.

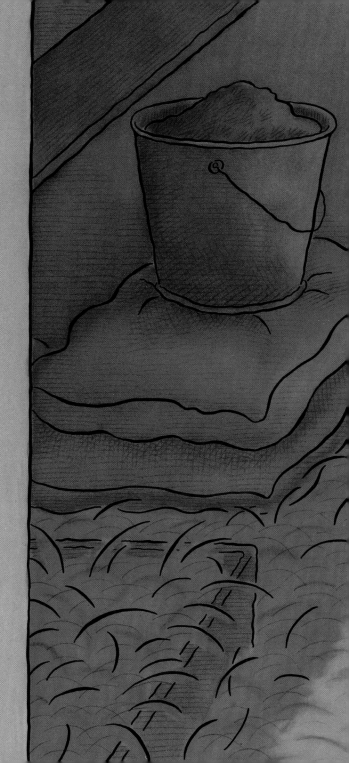

VIKING
Published by the Penguin Group
Viking Penguin, a division of Penguin Books USA Inc.,
345 Hudson Street, New York, New York 10014, U.S.A.
Penguin Books Ltd, 27 Wrights Lane, London W8 5TZ, England
Penguin Books Australia Ltd, Ringwood, Victoria, Australia
Penguin Books Canada Ltd, 10 Alcorn Avenue, Toronto, Ontario, Canada M4V 3B2
Penguin Books (N.Z.) Ltd, 182–190 Wairau Road, Auckland 10, New Zealand

Penguin Books Ltd, Registered Offices: Harmondsworth, Middlesex, England

First published in 1992 by Viking Penguin, a division of Penguin Books USA Inc.

20 19 18 17 16 15 14

Library of Congress Cataloging-in-Publication Data
Ernst, Lisa Campbell.
Zinnia and Dot / by Lisa Campbell Ernst.
p.   cm.
Summary: Zinnia and Dot, self-satisfied hens who bicker constantly about who lays
better eggs, put aside their differences to protect a prime specimen from a marauding weasel.
ISBN 0-670-83091-7
[1. Chickens—Fiction. 2. Eggs—Fiction. 3. Weasels—Fiction.] I. Title.
PZ7.E7323Z1   1992 [E]—dc20   91-36178   CIP   AC

Manufactured in China
Set in Goudy Old Style